From
Tree
to
Sea

Words by Shelley Moore Thomas

Art by Christopher Silas Neal

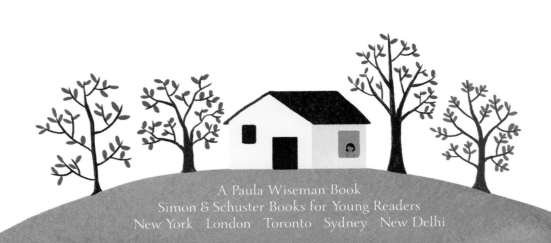

A Paula Wiseman Book
Simon & Schuster Books for Young Readers
New York   London   Toronto   Sydney   New Delhi

Earth shows me many things.

Trees show me how to stand tall.
Even when the wind
tries to blow me down,
I dance with the breeze.
I do not fall.

Stones show me how to be strong.
If I am kicked around sometimes,
like a rock in the road,
I just roll along.

Oceans show me how to travel far and wide.
I see all there is to see,

but I always return
with a friendly wave.

The sun shows me that brightness
brings warmth to others.
I smile and shine
when things look dim.

Clouds show me how to rise up
and float above problems.
I am so light,
I cannot be weighed down.

Bees show me how to work hard
and to help others.
When work is shared
the rewards are as sweet
as honey.

A baby bird shows me how not to be afraid
to spread my wings and fly.
I'll never find out how high
I can soar unless I try.

Soil shows me how to support those around me.
I care for tiny seeds until their roots are strong
and their leaves reach for the sky.
Good things can grow from me.

Cats show me how to be curious.
I playfully explore the world around me.
I study. I ponder. I learn.

Whales show me the wonder
of big things and small things.
I dream big dreams,
yet I can take only small strokes,
one at a time,
to make them come true.

The moon shows me that even when I change,
I am still me.
Sometimes it's round and pearly,
sometimes only a sliver,
but the moon is still the moon,
no matter what.
And I am always me,
no matter what.

What can the whale,
the stars,
the flower,
or the mountain
show you?

From dirt to cloud,
from sun to moon,
from tree to sea,
there is a wide and wonderful world out there,
waiting.

Just open your eyes.

You will find it.

To N., I., and C., who have taught me so much
–S. M. T.

For Jasper and River
–C. S. N.

SIMON & SCHUSTER BOOKS FOR YOUNG READERS
An imprint of Simon & Schuster Children's Publishing Division
1230 Avenue of the Americas, New York, New York 10020
Text copyright © 2019 by Shelley Moore Thomas · Illustrations copyright © 2019 by Christopher Silas Neal
SIMON & SCHUSTER BOOKS FOR YOUNG READERS is a trademark of Simon & Schuster, Inc.
For information about special discounts for bulk purchases, please contact Simon & Schuster
Special Sales at 1-866-506-1949 or business@simonandschuster.com.
The Simon & Schuster Speakers Bureau can bring authors to your live event. For more information or to book an event,
contact the Simon & Schuster Speakers Bureau at 1-866-248-3049 or visit our website at www.simonspeakers.com.
Book design by Chloë Foglia · The text for this book was set in Yana.
The illustrations for this book were rendered in mixed media and digital.
Manufactured in China
1118 SCP
First Edition
2 4 6 8 10 9 7 5 3 1
Library of Congress Cataloging-in-Publication Data
Names: Thomas, Shelley Moore, author. | Neal, Christopher Silas, illustrator.
Title: From tree to sea / Shelley Moore Thomas ; illustrated by Christopher Silas Neal.
Description: First edition. | New York : Simon & Schuster Books for Young Readers, [2018] | "A Paula Wiseman Book." |
Summary: Illustrations and easy-to-read text reveal lessons that nature teaches, such as how, like the sun,
one can bring warmth to others by smiling and shining even when things look dim.
Identifiers: LCCN 2018016739 | ISBN 9781481495318 (hardcover) | ISBN 9781481495325 (eBook)
Subjects: | CYAC: Nature–Fiction. | Conduct of life–Fiction.
Classification: LCC PZ7.T369453 Fro 2019 | DDC [E]–dc23
LC record available at https://lccn.loc.gov/2018016739